llama llama
mess, mess, mess

by **Anna Dewdney** and **Reed Duncan**
illustrated by **JT Morrow**

VIKING

Llama Llama in his room.
Cars and trucks go **HONK!** and ZOOM!
Racing under sheets and chairs . . .

Mama Llama calls upstairs.

Time to pick up all your toys!

Why is Mama making noise?

Mama says it's cleaning day. . . .
Llama only wants to **play**.

Mama says to make the bed.
Llama Llama shakes his head.

We all have a **job** to do—
even little llamas, too!

What if Mama *never* cleaned?
Imagine that!
What would that mean?

If Mama didn't dust or mop,
she'd toss the rags
and off she'd **hop**.

She'd take the clothes, all clean to wear,

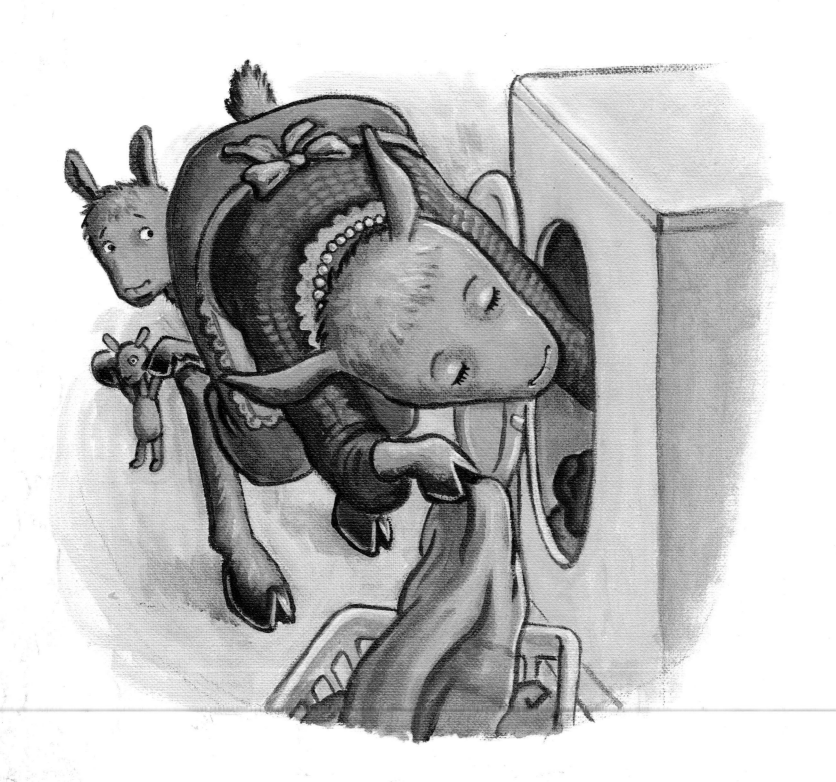

and **throw** them up into the air!

She'd pull the sheets right off the beds

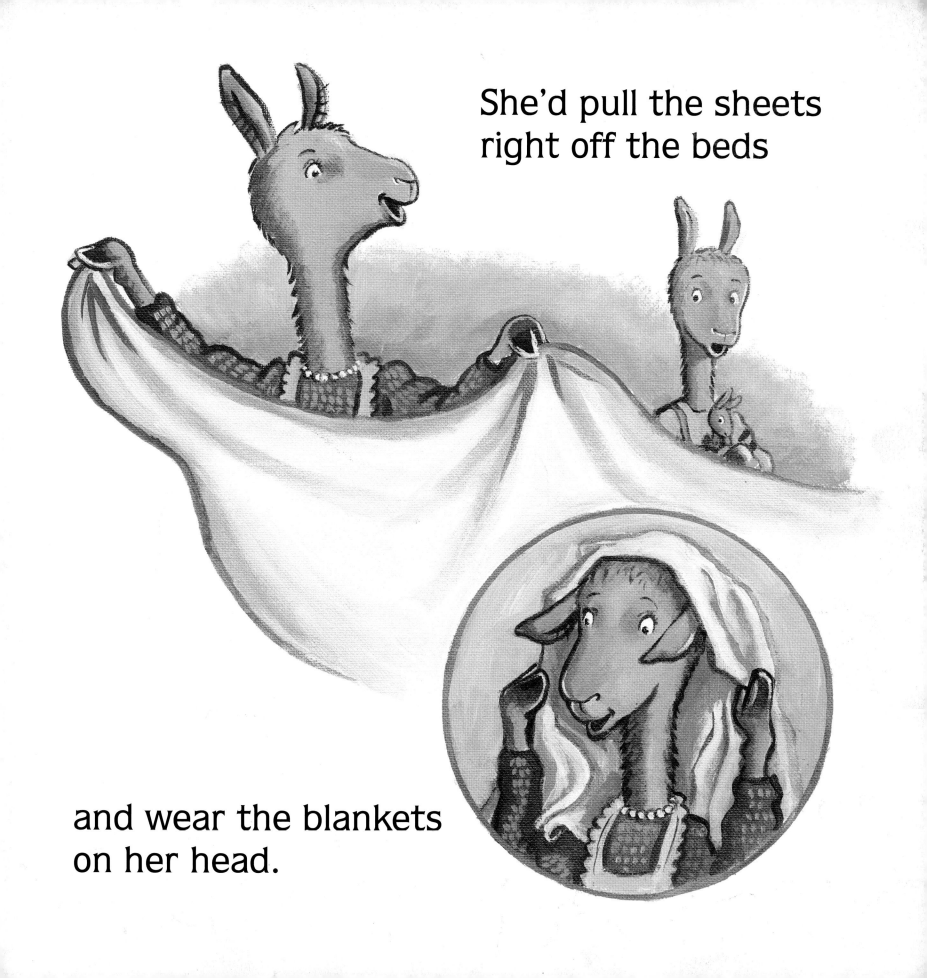

and wear the blankets on her head.

She'd leave the pots and pans and plates

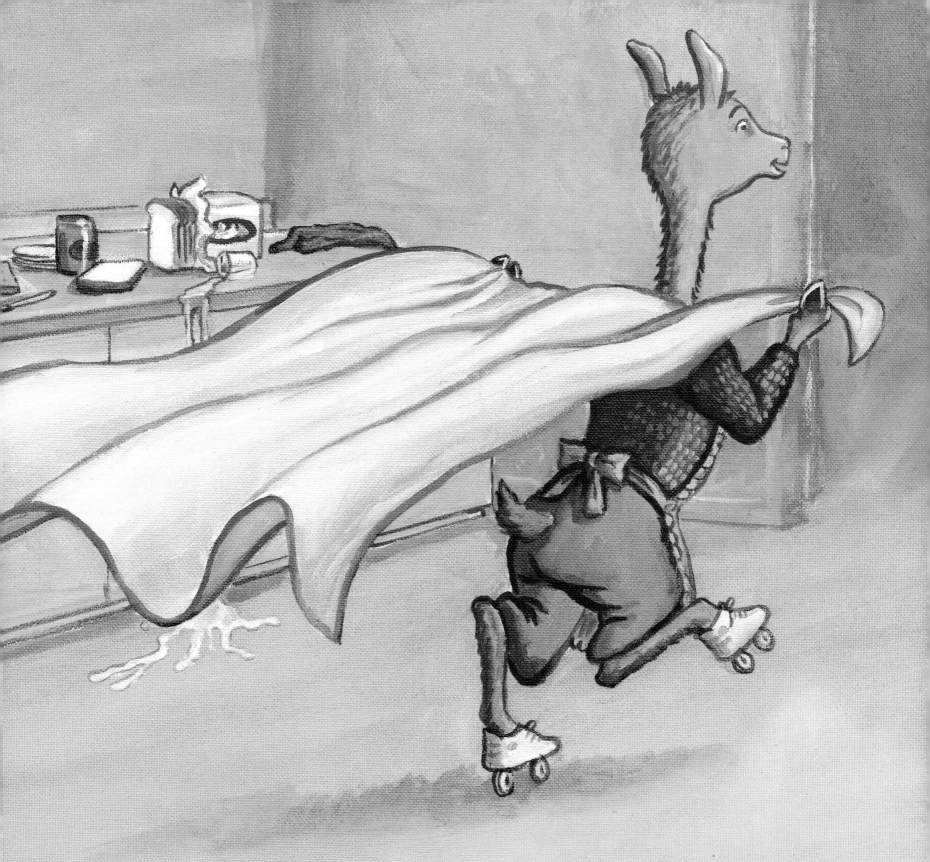

and dance around on roller skates.

Then **zoom** into the living room
to make a fort with mops and brooms.